Friends Go
Adventuring

First United States edition 1995

Margaret K. McElderry Books
An imprint of Simon & Schuster Children's Publishing Division
1230 Avenue of the Americas
New York, New York 10020

Copyright © 1994 by Diogenes Verlag AG, Zurich
English translation copyright © 1995 by Margaret K. McElderry Books, New York
First published in 1994 by Diogenes Verlag AG, Zurich

The text of this book is set in New Aster.
The illustrations were done in watercolor.

Printed in Germany

10 9 8 7 6 5 4 3 2 1

Library of Congress Catalog Card Number: 95-60367

ISBN 0-689-80463-6

Friends Go Adventuring

written and illustrated by

Helme Heine

Margaret K. McElderry Books

Today was like every other day on the farm.
The hens were hard at work because they had to lay a
thousand eggs. Charlie Rooster had to gather the eggs,
and it was more than he could manage.

The pigs on the farm were made to eat nonstop to
fatten them up. As soon as their plates were empty and
licked clean, they had to line up again for more food.
Though Fat Percy loved to eat, he thought this was *too* much.

Johnny Mouse was bored because the cat never had time to chase him anymore. Instead, the cat had to build mousetraps.

Every day the farmer plowed his field,
up and down, up and down on his tractor.

Nothing exciting ever happened on the farm. Everything
stayed the same. So the three friends—Charlie Rooster,
Fat Percy, and Johnny Mouse—set out in search of
adventure in the great, wide world.

Their first adventure happened right behind the hay field. There was the wily fox with six prisoners—the goose princess and her sisters. The brave friends freed the prisoners—and saved them from slavery or worse.

Soon after that, the friends found
Hugo, Milly the cow's youngest son.
He had gotten lost and was in
trouble, so they helped him.

Before long, it began to snow, but even in bad weather there can be adventures. Johnny Mouse discovered a big bottle with a message in it. The message read: TREASURE CHEST . . . ISLAND . . . RED SEA. At once, the three friends said, "We've got to find it!"

When they reached the Red Sea, they did find
the island. But before they got to it, a band
of pirates with a trained shark turned up.
The friends pedaled to the shore as fast as they
could and escaped just in time.

They rested in the shade of a palm tree.
While they weren't looking, a cannibal, who was
also a greedy cook, sneaked up and stole their bicycle.
He tried to catch them to put in his cooking pot.

The cannibal chased them right into the desert, but
there he—and the bicycle—gave up. Both of them ran
out of air. Hungry and tired, Charlie Rooster, Fat Percy,
and Johnny Mouse decided to go home to the farm.

On the way, they met Jumbo the elephant, who had heard about the three friends. He took them back by special delivery—just in time for dinner.

Before bedtime, the farmer and all the farm animals gathered behind the barn. Fat Percy, Charlie Rooster, and Johnny Mouse told their tales of princesses and pirates, snowstorms and deserts, of cannibals and buried treasure.

And also of . . . but that's another story!
True adventurers never run out of tales.